For Stephanie and Wendy
—N. S.

For Noah
—B. S

THE BABY HOUSE

BY NORMA SIMON

Illustrated by
BARBARA SAMUELS

SIMON & SCHUSTER BOOKS FOR YOUNG READERS

Once upon a time there were three mothers:

Louise,

Lassie,

and Mother.

There were three fathers, too:

Fuzzy,

Lance,

and Daddy.

And then there was me.

All the mothers wanted babies.
All the fathers wanted babies.
And I wanted all the babies.
All of us waited
        and waited
            and waited.

Louise grew rounder

and rounder

and rounder.

And I helped
Daddy make a
house for kittens.

The kittens came:

1   2   3   4

That's all.

Louise loved them, licked them, fed them.
All the mothers looked.
All the fathers looked.
And I looked.

All the mothers wanted babies.
All the fathers wanted babies.
And I wanted all the babies.
All of us waited
      and waited
         and waited.

Lassie grew rounder

and rounder

and rounder.

And I helped Daddy make
a house for puppies.

The puppies came:
1 2 3 4 5 6 7
That's all.
Lassie loved them, licked them, fed them.
All the mothers looked.
All the fathers looked.
And I looked.

All the mothers wanted babies.
All the fathers wanted babies.
And I wanted all the babies.
All of us waited
         and waited
                  and waited.

Mother grew rounder

and rounder

and rounder.

And I helped Daddy make
a new room for baby.

The baby came:
1
That's all.

Mother loved him,
kissed him, fed him.

And I helped Mother.

All the mothers looked.
All the fathers looked.
And I looked.

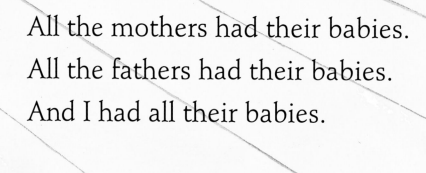

All the mothers had their babies.
All the fathers had their babies.
And I had all their babies.

We love them,
we kiss them,
we feed them.
We live in a baby house.

SIMON & SCHUSTER BOOKS FOR YOUNG READERS
1230 Avenue of the Americas, New York, New York 10020
Text copyright © 1995, 1955 by Norma Simon
Illustrations copyright © 1995 by Barbara Samuels
SIMON & SCHUSTER BOOKS FOR YOUNG READERS
is a trademark of Simon & Schuster.
Book design by Paul Zakris.
The text for this book is set in 21-point Stempel Schneidler.
The illustrations were done in watercolor.
Manufactured in the United States of America
10 9 8 7 6 5 4 3 2

Library of Congress Cataloging-in-Publication Data
Simon, Norma.   The baby house / by Norma Simon ;
illustrated by Barbara Samuels.   p.   cm.
Summary: A child tells how the family gets ready for
the birth of kittens, puppies, and a new baby.
[1. Babies—Fiction.   2. Cats—Fiction.   3. Dogs—Fiction.]
I. Samuels, Barbara, ill.   II. Title.
PZ7.S6053Bab   1995   [E]—dc20   94-6637   CIP AC
ISBN: 0-671-87044-0